CHAS WILLIAMSON

A Sweetheart Romance Novella

ROAD
to Paradise

Print ISBN:978-1-64649-249-7

eBook ISBN:978-1-64649-250-3

 Year of the Book
135 Glen Avenue
Glen Rock, PA 17327

Dedication

This title of this book is ironic. On that sunny summer day almost half a century ago, we took the first steps on our own road to paradise. And while there were detours and rough stretches along the way, I'm so proud I was the man who was lucky enough to be your partner. Hand-in-hand, we've blazed our own path. One thing's for sure, we did it our way. You and I, my love, we conquered the world, accomplishing things that now would seem impossible. Together, we created a home filled with love and happiness while we helped each other through college, created successful careers, designed and built our dream home, and made our fairy tale dreams a reality. I couldn't have dreamed up a better life, or more importantly, a better soulmate. But it wasn't just luck nor chance. God designed us for each other. And now that our life is entering a different phase, I'm not concerned. For with you by my side, I can do anything.

I love you forever, Janet Williamson.

Acknowledgments

Thank you, God, for creating love of all types, but especially romantic love.

Get exclusive
never-before-published content!

www.chaswilliamson.com

A Paradise Short Story

Download your free copy of
Skating in Paradise today

Chapter One

Now that summer had begun, the Paradise Bed and Breakfast was getting full. The inn had been open less than a month and so far, Beth loved her new job as hostess for the establishment. The routine was boring at times, but she met new people and was able to visit with her family almost daily.

Dropping another fresh linen-scented wax tart in the candle warmer in the sitting room, Beth replaced one of the books someone had removed from the shelf. Having read this one, Beth knew it was a love story set in World War II. With the lush, tropical South Pacific as the background, the couple fell in love, parted when he went back into action and then got together at the very end to live a happy life together. *Will I ever find a love like that?*

The soft whoosh of the front door broke her focus. A man's voice called out, "Anyone here?"

Walking from the room to the hallway, she encountered a young man, tall, thin and sporting curly, light-brown hair. His smile caught her attention. "May I help you?"

Gazing at her with steel blue eyes, he said, "Good afternoon. Do you work here?"

"Yes, I'm Beth Rutledge. May I be of assistance?"

"Uh, yes. My name is Anderson Warren. I'm staying in the area for a while, at a motel, and I just heard about this place. When I was a kid, we visited the Lancaster area and I have fond memories of the locale. I was wondering if you have any vacancies."

"Actually, we do. How long are you thinking of staying?"

The man hesitated before replying. "Between two and three months—most of the summer."

Beth's eyes took in his wide shoulders and muscular forearms. *Now that would be nice.* "Wow. I'll have to look, but I think we might be able to accommodate you. Let me grab my laptop and I'll be right back."

"Okay, I'll just hang out here."

He was really cute. "Come into the kitchen and have a seat." Beth led the young man into the dining area and motioned for him to take a chair at the table. She placed a plate and small tray of cookies in front of him. "I baked these this morning—chocolate chip oatmeal. They're from my mom's recipe." She pointed to the coffee maker that resided on the edge of the counter. "Please feel free to brew a cup of tea or coffee. Pods are in the cabinet below, as well as creamers. Excuse me for a moment."

She took one last glance at the man before heading up the stairs to the old master suite, which she used for her bedroom and office. Halfway up, a ping sounded on her phone, indicating a text message. Beth smiled as she read it. Her sister Missi wanted to know if Beth was coming over for dinner. *Of course!* Beth warmed as she thought of her sibling and family. *Glad I decided to stay in the area*. She texted back affirmatively before grabbing the computer and returning downstairs.

Anderson was sitting exactly where she'd left him. Glancing at the cookie tray, she noted he'd made quite a dent in the offering. He held up one of the treats. "You made these?"

Beth fought off a giggle. "Sure did."

"They are out of this world."

"Glad you like them. So how long did you want to stay?"

"Probably until the second week in August. I'm working in Reading and the project should be wrapped up by then."

"Here's what I have available..."

He agreed and gave her his information. She provided him with a quick tour before he left. "After I check out of the other establishment, I'll be back."

She couldn't help but smile. *This job does have its perks*. Hopefully, she'd get to know Mr. Warren a little better.

***

The table was packed with Beth's three younger sisters, her mom, and baby brother, all making noise at once. The man she now called her dad, Sam Espenshade, used a cane to walk but carried a heaping pan of sausage and potatoes by the handle. His bad leg was the result of standing up to a bully who tried to assault her mom. Sam set the pan beside a pot of peas and carrots that was already in place.

"Hey, there's Beth. My favorite oldest daughter." Sam gave her a brief hug and a peck on the cheek.

"Want me to dish out the food?"

Her mom, Hannah, smiled at her. "Thanks, sweetie." She turned to her husband as the timer sounded from the kitchen. "Don't forget the rolls."

Sam returned to the kitchen while Beth filled the plates.

Her sister, Missi, also ran into the kitchen. "I'll help you with the drinks, Daddy."

Hannah turned to her. "How's life at the B&B?"

"We're almost full. A gentleman from Cincinnati booked a room today. He'll be staying with us for a couple of months."

Beth caught the way her mom raised her eyebrow. "That's good. How old is he?"

She could feel her face heat. "Late twenties, maybe." *And really, really handsome.*

"What's he do?"

"Anderson told me he's a geologist."

"What in the world would a geologist be doing in Lancaster?"

Beth replaced the ladle in the pan at the same time Sam and Missi returned. "He works for an environmental firm. They're doing some sort of project in Reading."

When everyone was seated, Sam offered grace and then asked. "Who's doing a project in Reading?"

Beth caught the sly smile and wink her mom sent to her step-dad. "One of the guests."

Hannah's voice had a teasing inflection. "He's in his twenties."

Missi put down her glass. "Is he cute?" Now that Missi was a teenager, all she seemed to think about was boys.

It was getting warm. "Kind of."

Sam passed the rolls to Beth. "Kind of? It sounds like an interesting blend of guests there. A photographer, an author and now... an engineer."

"Geologist, Dad," Missi corrected.

Sam got that crooked smile on his face, the one Beth loved. "Geologist. Maybe he's looking for a vein of gold... or some other treasure."

He was also picking on her, she knew. Beth decided to change the subject. "I was wondering if I could borrow a couple of movies."

"Still watching nightly movies in the hot tub, huh?" her mom asked.

Henry and Ellie Campbell had moved Hannah and her girls in with the Campbell family after Kyle Parker attacked her mom. Back before Hannah married Sam. During the two months they'd stayed there, many a night was spent watching Blu-rays with the combined families in the hot tub downstairs.

"Yep. Terry and Eileen watch them with me almost every night."

Sam harumphed. "Let's hope your new tenant doesn't decide to join you."

Again, she could feel her face heat. "Dad, puh-lease. You act like I've never been around boys. I am twenty-one, you know."

"And you're still my baby."

Hannah laughed. "And mine as well. Your driver's license may say twenty-one, but I believe deep inside you've got the wisdom of a lady twice your age. I have every faith you'll put that insight to use by making good choices."

Beth could guess what they were thinking, that she was a starry-eyed kid who wasn't wise to the ways of the world.

"You taught me well, both of you. Maybe that's why I came home instead of staying on full-time at the resort in Florida. I did have a great job offer there, remember?"

Hannah again smiled. "I'm so glad you decided to come back to Lancaster. Hmm... a good movie? Sam and I watched *Rat Race* last week. You could take that, unless you want one of the scary dinosaur movies. They used to be your favorites."

Not when I'm staying by myself. The thought of dinosaurs feasting on humans now gave her nightmares. "*Rat Race* would be fine. Do you have any goodies I can take with me?"

"They're already packed. By the way, Missi and I are making fried chicken tomorrow. Will you be joining us?"

Her mom could have continued the teasing, but one thing Beth knew... her parents trusted her, totally. And she'd never do anything to let them down. "Wouldn't miss family time for the world. Want some help cleaning up?"

Hannah's smile was back. "No. Go and have fun tonight."

Sam scowled but Beth knew it was all for show. "Just not *too* much fun."

Chapter Two

Anderson had just finished unpacking his belongings when his phone sounded. Glancing at the screen, he saw it was a text and immediately knew it was from Michaela, his ex-girlfriend.

U busy? Hoping we could talk. Miss U bunches.

He didn't bother to respond. After what he'd caught Michaela doing, he had no desire to *ever* talk to her again. Anderson had blocked her cell, but this text was from a different number. *Why can't I find a girl who has the same dreams as I do?* Was a loving and monogamous, life-long relationship too much to ask for?

Anderson shook his head to drive the girl from his mind. It was about seven-thirty. The hostess had told him there was a hot tub in the basement and several of the guests hung out there in the evening, just watching movies. After the day he'd had, Anderson felt the need to relax.

At the last motel, Michaela had discovered where he'd been staying and had constantly harassed him with messages left at the front desk. And when the busy-body desk clerk put in her two cents' worth and insisted he should talk to Michaela, that's when Anderson decided to change where he slept at night.

He slipped into his trunks and threw on a Cincinnati Reds t-shirt. The room had plenty of towels, so he took one along and walked down to the basement. There were three women in the spa.

Beth was there, along with two of the female guests. After a brief glance, his eyes returned to his hostess. He had to blink twice to make sure it was only his imagination, but he could swear he'd seen a sparkle in her eyes.

He eased into the hot tub, right next to Beth.

"Hi, Anderson."

He gave her what he hoped was a pleasant smile, the opposite of what his mood was like inside. "Evening, Beth. You can call me Andy if you'd like."

Beth introduced him to the two women—Terry the writer and Eileen the photographer. With that done, Beth repositioned to face him and then shook her head while she was laughing. "What is a geologist doing in Lancaster? Is there a new fault line or are you investigating a recent earthquake?"

"No, I work for an environmental company and we're cleaning up an old industrial site."

"Cool. Speaking of geology, there are some caves in the area. I'd be glad to act as a tour guide."

Anderson couldn't take his eyes off her beautiful face, not even if he'd wanted to. The sparkle in her eyes made his chest feel funny. "That might be nice. I do love spelunking, so maybe this weekend?"

"I'd really like that." The girl's smile was increasing his pulse rate.

"I like caves as well." The horror-author Terry had broken the spell. "I didn't know you gave tours."

Like I'd want to go anywhere with you. His grandfather would have been proud of how he'd simply smiled and kept his mouth shut.

Beth faced the woman, but her skin color seemed to pale. "Well, uh, sure. When we moved to Lancaster, my step-dad Sam took us to see all the... how did he put it? Oh yes, I remember. The tourist spots. I could do that." She glanced at the photographer—Eileen, he recalled. "We could all go."

Even though the girl offered, Anderson knew the invitation had been for him, not them. *She likes me.* Maybe it was a good thing Terry had interrupted and allowed his pulse rate to return to normal. Anderson would have to be careful. His heart was still tender from Michaela's betrayal and the last thing he wanted to do was to pass that pain to someone else, especially someone as sweet as his hostess.

***

The enticing scent of bacon tickled his nose. *Glad I changed lodging.* The hostess sure knew how to cook. He had to leave by five-thirty on weekdays and the girl had something ready for him each morning. The young lady also went out of her way and packed treats from her mother's bakery for a mid-day snack. He closed his eyes for another moment and a face appeared before him—Beth's. So pure and kind, not to mention pretty. Anderson knew he was smiling.

There were other reasons why he liked staying here, besides the cooking and Beth's company. He'd struck up a friendship with the photographer Eileen, though her crazy author friend Terry still bothered him. He'd joined the trio for a second night to watch movies in the spa, but Terry's constant flirting and off-the-wall comments reminded him of Michaela and her coquettish actions. For the rest of the week, he'd spent his evenings reading or watching ball games on the television in his room.

But today was Saturday, and hopefully he'd spend a lot of it with Beth. After a quick shower, he headed down to breakfast. At the bottom of the stairs, he almost ran into Beth. Her arms were laden with a tray of plates full of scrambled eggs, bacon and cinnamon rolls. Like Pavlov's dog, his mouth began to water.

"I was wondering if you were going to join us." The girl's smile made him warm.

"Sorry, I enjoyed sleeping in."

There was an understanding in her eyes. "You work way too hard." It seemed Beth was going to say something else, but didn't.

"Want a hand taking the tray outside?"

"No, but you can do me a favor."

"Sure, what's that?"

A slight pink appeared on her cheeks. "There's two plates on the counter in the kitchen. Can you get those?"

"Absolutely. Who are they for?"

"You and me." Beth darted for the front door.

You and me? That confirmed the interest was mutual. Anderson couldn't wait for the meal to conclude because, after breakfast, he and the three women would be heading to Crystal Cave in Kutztown. But his mind wasn't contemplating going into a cavern. Instead, Anderson was wondering what it would feel like to hold Beth's hand. *Stop this!*

After what seemed to be decades, the young woman stood and collected her dishes. "I'm going to load the dishwasher." Beth turned to Anderson. "What time are we thinking about leaving?"

"How about in half an hour? I don't mind driving, but I'll need to move my gear to the back to free up the rear seat." Anderson also got to his feet. "Let me give you a hand with those, Beth."

"That's sweet, but I've got it."

Anderson ignored what she'd said and grabbed the serving tray. "My grandpa used to say, many hands make light work, so you're stuck with me." He heaped dirty plates onto the serving platter and followed Beth into the kitchen.

As Anderson stood, waiting for Beth to place the dirty dishes into the dishwasher, he noticed her smile. "What's so funny?"

"I know for certain why you followed me in here."

"Uh, what do you mean?"

"You were afraid."

Huh? "I'm not following you."

Beth giggled. "Oh yes you did, follow me that is, and I thank you for that."

She's not only cute, she's funny. "My pleasure. What do you think I was afraid of?"

"Terry. I swear her picture has to be in the dictionary next to the word annoying."

The two shared a brief laugh before the girl's face turned serious. "She likes you, in case you didn't know."

"Well, it's not reciprocated."

Beth started the dishwasher and turned to face him. The smile on her face was enchanting. "I know that."

***

There was one benefit of sitting in the rear seat. Beth didn't have to turn her head to see Anderson's face. It was before her in the mirror. And the second advantage was she could see every time he glanced her way, which was quite often.

Sitting in the passenger seat, Eileen raised her camera to capture the image of a pair of Amish workhorses standing in a pasture. Eileen ended up in the shotgun seat because Terry insisted. Terry had argued it would make it easier for her friend to photograph anything interesting they came upon from that vantage point.

"Is the temperature okay back there?"

Beth gazed at the mirror and found Anderson staring at her. Those steel blue eyes seemed to be smiling at her.

"It's okay," Terry answered even though Beth knew the question had been directed at her. "Are we there yet?" *Must be the thirtieth time she'd asked the same question.*

The man's eyes returned to the road briefly. "No, we're not there yet." He searched the mirror until he had Beth's attention. "How about you, *Beth*

Rutledge?" Anderson accented her name to remove any doubt as to whom he was addressing.

The obvious caring in his expression made it very warm in the back seat. "It's fine. This is a nice, comfy vehicle."

Anderson laughed. "Oh, it's just a rental. I like the roominess, but it's not my style."

"Hmm. What kind of car do you have?"

"A Dodge Challenger."

"Why would you want one of those?" Terry asked. "They're gas hogs. Wait, I know. You have it so you can pick up girls."

Beth noted the red on Anderson's cheeks. Terry annoyed him, but the man was always pleasant. "My grandfather has one of the originals—a 1970. Still runs. He and I spent many a weekend riding around in that vehicle. He bought it new and after I paid off my college loans, I followed suit and bought a new one myself."

That was the second time today that Anderson had mentioned his grandfather. "Sounds like you and your granddad are close."

"He and Nana practically raised me. My mom is the regional manager for a large chain of fast-food restaurants. She spends a lot of time on the road. Guess that's why my dad split when I was young. After their divorce, mom moved us in with her parents. They became my surrogate parents and mom was more like an aunt who came to visit every other weekend."

Terry's voice was softer now and lacked the teasing quality she usually used. "Sorry to hear that.

And now your job has you on the road a lot. I hope for your sake that history doesn't repeat itself."

Beth couldn't read the reaction on Anderson's face, but she did note how his vision was focused on the road ahead. "Not a chance on that. When I find the right girl, I'm settling down. Mom tried, but she allowed her career to be her passion." His head turned and his eyes locked on Beth's. "My passion will be my family and the woman who one day becomes my wife."

Chapter Three

B eth took a deep breath, taking in the scent of the fresh cut hay that filled the car, the fields, all the air. "We're almost there. Turn right at the next stop sign." Anderson was again playing chauffeur, but this time, Beth had the honor of riding shotgun. Earlier, the man took action and held the front passenger door for Beth before Terry could reach the vehicle. Eileen had decided to ride with Josh Miller and his kids in a large pickup behind them.

Anderson had a glow about him this morning. "I'm so excited to ride on the Strasburg Railroad. My grandparents took me here when I was maybe five. I've loved trains ever since."

Terry's comment drifted from the back. "Sounds like the little boy part of you never matured. That's a plot characteristic I've used in some of my books. A child whose youthful fantasies never developed, then he turned evil..." The woman continued to drone on for the remainder of the ride.

Anderson shook his head slightly. Terry meant no harm, but Beth could tell the horror writer's personality grated on him. Despite that, he was always kind to the author. *A trait of a true gentleman.* That's what her mom had said when Beth told her about Anderson and Terry.

"Oh wow, look at that!" They had just pulled into the parking lot and Anderson was pointing at a big locomotive, white, puffy smoke billowing from her stack. "That's a Baldwin 2-10-0."

Terry yawned from the back seat. "Looks like a train to me."

The excitement on his face was contagious. They were out of the vehicle now. Beth was trying to keep up as he took in the sight. "What is a... what did you say, two by ten something or other?"

Those steel blue eyes seemed to be on fire. "A man named Frederick Whyte developed a classification system for steam locomotives. Two is the number of leading wheels, ten refers to those powered by the engine, and zero is the number of trailing wheels. That lady," he pointed to the engine, "is also called a *decapod* and she's a beauty."

Terry stood at Beth's right side and whispered loud enough for Beth to pick up on her words, "Most men only get this excited over bipods of the feminine variety."

Josh Miller's truck arrived and the children spilled out. The boy, Dakota, was wide-eyed. "Holy cow! A real steam engine. I didn't know they still made them."

Beth was touched by the way Anderson knelt down to face the child. "Don't let her looks fool you. She was built in 1924 in Philadelphia by the greatest locomotive builder in the world—Baldwin. This old girl spent most of her life on the Great Western Railroad before Strasburg acquired her in '67."

Anderson took the little boy's hand and together the two approached the steam locomotive for a closer look.

Terry nudged her elbow into Beth's ribs. "Wonder if he googles the women he dates with the same enthusiasm, you know... to get background information on them as well."

"I think it's cool. Look at how passionate he is. And how he's sharing that love of trains with Dakota."

The horror writer turned and faced Beth, a knowing smile covering her face. "You like him, don't you?"

Despite being used to Terry's directness, Beth felt her face heat. "H-he's very nice."

"Um-hmm. And quite attractive. I saw how you checked him out that evening when we were watching *Rat Race*. He looked nice in those swim trunks, don't you think? I see the beginning of a plot forming here..."

Enough. "Not everything is a story for one of your books."

Terry took a step backwards. "I meant no harm. When you're an author, you just see everything in a different way, that's all. You look for—"

"Then don't look," Beth cut her off. "Anderson is my friend and I don't appreciate the negative comments, or, or... just quit running him down, please?"

Terry laughed. "Okay. You've got it. I think I'll go talk to Eileen now." With that, the woman turned and left Beth standing alone. But not for long. Anderson came running back to her.

"Would you like to come with me?" He extended his hand. "I'll explain all about how the locomotive works. Please?"

With such an excited look on his face, how could a girl resist? Even if it was about a chunk of metal. "Sure." She reached out and took the young man's hand.

He led her to the big black engine and pointed to the car behind it. "Now, this is the tender. The tender carries the fuel for the engine. In this case, we're burning coal."

Beth was impressed by his obvious knowledge, but that wasn't what had her attention. Instead, it was his hand. He hadn't released hers, even after they stood at the front of the train. The warmth that started there continued to flow into every part of her body, especially her heart. He kept talking about how the device worked, putting it into plain English in a way that wasn't like a scientific lecture, but rather layman's terms. The tone of his voice was soothing. *I could listen to you for hours on end...*

"All aboard!" the conductor yelled.

Still hand-in-hand, they caught up with the crowd and climbed aboard an open-aired passenger car. Eileen, Josh, Terry and the kids occupied the center section of the coach. Anderson's hand was still entwined with hers.

"You can sit with me." It was Terry. "I'll move over."

Anderson faced Beth and spoke so only she could hear. "I'd like to sit in the dining car, if that's all right with you."

The sparkle in those blue eyes couldn't be missed. *I'll follow you anywhere...* But all she could get out was, "Yes."

The man turned to Terry and replied, "I know the food section's not open right now, but I think we'll sit in the dining car. It's a genuine Pullman, after all." He hesitated then added, "You can join us if you like."

Beth was watching Terry. The woman reached for the seatback and Beth knew she'd be following along... until Eileen loudly cleared her throat. The annoyed expression Terry shot at her friend almost made Beth giggle.

Terry frowned. "I think the air might be a little stuffy in there. I'll ride in this car."

"Okay, we'll see you in a little." Anderson quickly led the way into the dining car.

Because of the outside temperature, Terry was correct. It was almost stifling inside. They had the dining car all to themselves. The man led her to two plush and deeply cushioned seats, which swiveled and allowed them to take in the scenery. "Are you sure this is okay? I know it's pretty warm in here."

Was the ambient air or his hand, which still held hers, the reason why she felt so warm? "I'm good." After they sat down, she felt his hand tremble. "Andy, I've never seen you this excited. Why?"

The coach lurched as the train started moving, but instead of looking outside the window, his full attention was focused on her. "Probably not what you think. Yes, I love railroads and eating in a dining car is on my bucket list, but... look, don't think I'm weird, but I, I really like you. I was trying to find a way to ask you out or something. It's just that I'm kind of shy and..." His face was red and she was sure it wasn't from the oppressive heat.

She squeezed his hand. "I like you, too. Thank you for taking me along this morning."

"The pleasure is all mine. It seems your friends are always around and I believe that writer woman's goal in life is to make fun of me, every step I take."

"That she does. But don't worry."

Anderson wrinkled his nose before speaking. "About what?"

"What she says doesn't matter. I may be young, but I'm mature enough that I don't pay attention to what my friends say. I draw my own conclusions. That's something my mom taught me how to do."

There was amusement on his face. "Oh yeah? Sounds like your mom's kind of cool. But I'm curious. What would they be? Your conclusions, I mean."

Beth swallowed hard, hoping he hadn't noticed. This was new territory and her comments had been a bit of a bluff. She took her time answering. "This, this is exactly where I want to be."

"You like being in this hot train car?"

A giggle slipped out. She lifted his hand. "No, I was referring to this."

***

The day was turning out to exceed even his wildest dreams. Anderson was attracted to Beth and thought she was kind of cool, but as the day continued, his heart seemed to race faster than his mind. The thought of what her lips might taste like intrigued him, very, very much.

"Is Harrisburg the capital of Pennsylvania?"

Anderson almost forgot Terry had tagged along.

Beth's voice came from the passenger seat. "Yes. The capitol building is only a short walk from the museum. If you want, we can go see it after our visit."

"Maybe. Sounds more interesting than walking around looking at rocks."

From the corner of his eye, he noted how Beth glanced his way and winked. This trip had been Beth's suggestion—to visit the Pennsylvania State Museum. Beth knew he wanted to spend more time at both the Railroad Museum and the big model train layout at the Choo-Choo Barn in Strasburg, but she'd quietly suggested they could do it some other time—when Terry wasn't along. Anderson suspected Beth's proposition had more to do with dissuading Terry from tagging along. But the writer was like a self-appointed chaperone.

Terry's voice lacked enthusiasm. "What exhibit are we visiting first?"

Beth quickly answered, "The Hall of Geology."

"Great. Every girl's dream," Terry groused loudly.

Beth shot him a wide smile and spoke just loud enough for Anderson to hear, "Then maybe she should have stayed home."

The majority of the afternoon was spent on the museum's third floor, checking out the Life Through Time, which had one of the most complete Mastodon skeletons in the world. Terry found a place to sit and interface with her cell phone, but Beth hung close to his side.

"I never would have guessed this kind of stuff would interest you."

Terry was no longer in view and Anderson was surprised when she took his hand. "I was really into the whole Jurassic Park kind of thing when I was younger. So yes, this does interest me." She squeezed his hand briefly. "Among other things."

They strolled in silence, fingers interlaced, to Mammal Hall. A family, with several young children, was walking a little farther ahead.

"It's cool that those parents brought their kids here. Most youths today would rather go to an amusement park instead of seeing something like this. My grandparents did a good job mixing the two. Because of them, I had a happy childhood."

"I'm sorry you're not close with your mom. Mine is my best friend. Corny, I know, but I spend more time with her than anyone else."

"She sounds like a gem."

Beth took a deep breath. "That she is. So is my step-dad, Sam."

"I hope someday you'll take me to meet them. As time goes by, I'd like to learn more about you."

Beth stopped and turned Anderson so they were face-to-face. "How old are you?"

"Twenty-nine, and you?"

There was a smile on her lips. "Want to guess?"

Now there was a hot potato. "My thought is you are... perfect for any age."

Beth giggled. "Great answer. But remember this... age is simply a number. In years, I'm twenty-one."

Whoops. Thought you were closer to my age. "You seem quite mature for a girl so young."

The way she nibbled on her lip drew his attention. "People mature at different levels. Andy, my dad, well... step-dad, is two years younger than you. And he's twelve years younger than Mom. But God intended for them to be together. You need to know I believe God has a purpose for everything."

He ignored the theological comment. "That's a huge difference in age. Do they get along well?"

Beth's eyes seemed to study his. "They're poster children for true love."

"Few people believe in true love today."

"Well, I do. I've seen it first-hand."

"Really? What do they have in common?"

"Everything. You see, my real dad died before we moved here. Sam worked with Mom and became her friend, her best friend. Sam spent lots of time with us, introducing our family to the area. He tailored his life to fit ours. What was important to us became what mattered most to him. He was filled with a devotion to our family that was undeniable. So deep that he almost gave his life to save mine."

A chill rolled across Anderson's shoulders. The result of the air-conditioner kicking on or... something else? "Are you speaking figuratively or..."

For the next ten minutes, Beth described how her step-father almost died to save not only Beth, but her sister Missi from a burning building.

Anderson was moved by the story, but the reveal seemed random. "Why did you tell me this today?"

"Hey, you guys! Wait up." Terry was approaching.

Beth's gaze burned a path through his eyes directly to his heart. "I really like you. I shared this with you because what I described, that's the kind of love I want. The kind God intended for me to have. Before we go any farther, I wanted you to know my desires."

Chapter Four

T he shrill ring of the cell interrupted the wonderful dream. He and Beth had been walking hand-in-hand in a field of daisies until...

The disembodied voice belonged to Melvin, the security guard working the site in Reading. "Mr. Warren, hate to bother you, but we got a problem."

Glancing at the clock next to the bed revealed it was quarter of four on Sunday morning. "What's wrong?"

"There's a water leak coming from the ceiling, right over that stack of drums."

"The closed or open drums?"

"Open ones, sir."

"Great, I'm on my way. See if you can figure out how to shut off the water. Be there soon."

When he'd departed on Friday, the crew left the lids off about twenty drums they were in the process of filling. Any water that landed in and then overflowed from the drums would be contaminated.

He needed his workers to come in and address the problem. As he drove, he used the hands-free feature to try and contact the crew. He was on site almost an hour before finally reaching one of the crew leaders.

Luckily, Melvin and Anderson were able to shut off the water, but the entire site was a mess. The previously remediated lower level now had two feet of standing water. Not knowing if the basement was water-tight, he directed the crew to pump out the water and clean up the mess. The project was still in process, but manageable when Anderson finally left at two in the afternoon.

As he pointed the SUV toward Lancaster, two thoughts flowed through his mind. First, he needed a shower in the worst way, but more importantly, he needed to talk to Beth. Her confession about the type of relationship she was looking for floored him. It was as if the lady had read his mind. When they finally got back to the B&B last night and ditched Terry, there had been a couple who wanted to speak with her. While waiting, Anderson turned on a ball game. But instead of watching it in his room, he turned on the TV in the setting room and waited for her. Unfortunately, Beth never showed.

The text alert on his cell went off. *Please be Beth.*

Hi sweetie,

Miss U.

R U coming home or should I stop by? Want to show U my new bikini.

Can't wait to C U!

Anderson threw the device on the floor. "Great. Can anything else go wrong today?"

***

After helping clear the lunch plates, Beth stepped out onto the porch and parked herself in the glider. This had been her place of solace when she was younger. Whether it was homework, reading a book or talking with friends on the phone, much of her youthful life in Lancaster had been spent on the old metal swing. The screen door closed and Beth looked up. Her mother, Hannah, carried two glasses of iced tea.

"Hey, baby. What's going on?"

"Nothing, Mom."

"Okay. Mind if I sit with you, for old time's sake?"

"I'd like that."

The older woman handed Beth the beverage. Two open-topped Amish buggies clip-clopped by. The first held a teenaged couple who stiffly focused their attention on the road ahead. The second contained a young man and two girls. While the younger of the two sat next to the driver, the second was sitting on the floorboard, facing the pair.

Hannah giggled. "Looks like someone has a chaperone."

Not really meaning for her mother to hear it, Beth muttered, "I know the feeling."

Hannah set down her glass and turned to Beth. "Would you like to talk about it?"

Beth's gaze followed the buggies until they disappeared around a bend in the road. "How do you know there's something to talk about?"

Hannah put an arm around her and drew her in, lips brushing the top of Beth's head. "Because I know you better than anyone. I held you first. I'm not just your mom, I'm your friend, and always will be."

A sigh escaped her chest. "I overstepped yesterday."

"Really? How?"

"I made the mistake of telling Anderson what I wanted."

"Which was?"

It felt so comforting to be held by Hannah, bringing back memories of when Beth was little and Mommy's touch could make everything all better. "I told him I wanted what you and Sam have. I wanted to be loved like that."

Brief silence. "What did he say?"

"We were at the museum and Terry interrupted before he could answer. That woman annoys me to no end, but, like you told me, smother your enemies with kindness."

"What did the writer say now?"

"Nothing in particular. She was just being Terry. On the way back from Harrisburg, we stopped for ice cream, then came back to the B&B."

"Did you and Anderson talk when you returned to the inn?"

"No-o. One of the other guests wanted information about the area. By the time I finished with them, Andy was engrossed in some baseball game on TV. I didn't want to interrupt him, so I went to bed."

"I'm sorry."

"Then this morning, his car was gone before I got up. He wasn't there for breakfast." Beth sniffed to clear her nose.

Hannah drew her deeper into her arms. "*Shh.* It will be all right."

"I should have kept my big mouth shut. I think he got scared by what I said."

"Shush, honey. If that's the type of man he is, then it's better to know that now before you fall too hard."

A fly landed on Beth's arm and she shooed it away. "It still hurts. I really thought he might be the one."

Hannah again kissed her head before releasing Beth. "I suspected as much."

Beth turned to search her mother's face. "Why can't I find someone like you did? Someone who loves me with the intensity Sam loves you? Someone I can devote my life to?"

Hannah touched her cheek. "It will happen. Remember, it's not on our time schedule, it's God's."

Leaning back against the glider, Beth looked to the skies. "I wish He'd hurry."

***

The afternoon seemed to drag on. Beth still occupied the glider, but shared it with Missi. Beneath their feet, her two youngest sisters, Jenna and Angie, were playing with blocks.

"Thanks for painting my nails." Missi lifted her hand so she could check out her newly-painted fingertips.

"No problem. That's what sisters do." After Beth closed the lid, she watched her younger siblings for a moment.

Missi broke the solitude. "Thanks for always taking time to play with me when I was a kid. I know you didn't have to."

"My pleasure. You still are... a kid, that is."

"Am not. I'm in my teens." A brief pause. "I miss you living here. Even though Mom and Dad let me have your old room, every time I walk into it, I expect you to be there."

Beth reached for her sister's hand and squeezed it. "I live just down the road, silly."

"I know, but it's not the same as having my big sister with me all the time."

"Good thing I didn't take the job in Florida, huh?"

Missi smiled. "I don't know. We could have gone to the parks every day."

Laughter. "That got old, quickly. If Mom and Dad don't mind, maybe you could stay with me for a few days."

"Do I have to help you do stuff?"

"That's part of the deal."

The screen door opened and their parents walked out. Sam held the baby in his arms. Her step-dad's smile was ear-to-ear. "Guess who woke up in time to see his big sisters?"

"Hey, Sammy Junior. How's my little bro?"

The little boy rubbed his eyes. Hannah extracted a plastic bag with some crackers from her pocket and handed it to her husband. "I bet someone is hungry. Here, Daddy. Why don't you give your son a snack?"

Beth winked at Missi. "You know, I'm getting a little hungry as well. I saw there were whoopie pies on the counter. Maybe you could sneak in and grab us some... before Mom knows they're missing."

Hannah laughed. "They're for dessert. Sam's going to cook burgers and sausage for supper. Then you can have your choice of fresh peach cobbler or the snack pies."

Missi's eyes lit up. "Can he make us corn on the grill?" She turned to face the man. "Please... Daddy?"

Beth shook her head. Ever since she'd known Sam, Missi had him wrapped around her finger. Despite the sadness in her heart, Beth could sense something very comforting here, in this place. She quickly identified it—love.

The sound of tires rolling on stone got everyone's attention. A large black SUV stopped in their lane.

Sam spoke out loud. "I wonder who this could be?" He exchanged a look with his wife. Beth couldn't read the unspoken communication.

But Beth knew the vehicle. She'd ridden in it—just yesterday. Her mouth was dry as the young man stepped out and then opened the rear door. Her heart threatened to beat out of her chest as he moved onto the walk. The man's arm was behind his back as he approached. He nodded at her parents before speaking.

"Good afternoon. You must be Mr. and Mrs. Espenshade."

Sam handed the baby to Hannah. "That we are. And who are you?"

His eyes finally found Beth's. "I'm Anderson Warren and," he pulled a large bouquet of flowers from behind his back, "I came to call on Beth."

Chapter Five

Two tractor trailers were lumbering side by side on Route 222 South, both ten miles below the speed limit. Anderson shook his head. "Come on, get a move on. Gas pedal's on the right." He'd missed breakfast. Beth probably thought he skipped out intentionally. Anderson needed to make her understand he totally understood and agreed with what she told him. The kind of love Beth described was *exactly* what he wanted.

Arriving back at the inn, the first thing he noticed was that Beth's Explorer was missing. "Probably visiting with her parents." After a quick shower he ran outside, but then realized he had no clue where they lived. "Now what?" He momentarily considered asking Terry, but she'd want to tag along, so that option was a no-go.

Laughter from the backyard next door caught his attention. A gathering of some sort was going on. Glancing at the group, he recognized the pretty woman with jet-black hair and dimples on her cheek and chin. It was Ellie Campbell. Anderson had met her once or twice. Ellie owned the B&B. It took courage, but he forced himself to walk over and introduce himself. The black-haired woman was talking to a beautiful blonde lady who sported an English accent. When Anderson explained he wished to know where Beth lived and confessed why, the two women laughed. But Ellie immediately gave him Beth's parents' address.

After stopping to buy a bouquet of roses, Anderson pointed his ride to Strasburg and found the Espenshade home. It sat right next to a block structure that sported a sign declaring "Hannah's Bakery."

He stepped out of the Suburban. *Legs, quit shaking.* Anderson hid the bouquet behind his back. All eyes were on him as he entered the yard. A man stood, baby in his arm, yet balancing himself with a cane. He looked much younger than Anderson expected. A very classy lady with strawberry-blonde hair and green eyes stood next to the man. She appeared to be assessing him. But the thing that concerned him the most was Beth's expression. His friend sure didn't look happy he was here.

Anderson swallowed hard before speaking. "Good afternoon. You must be Mr. and Mrs. Espenshade."

The man handed the baby to the woman and moved onto the steps. Anderson couldn't help but notice how hard he leaned on the cane. "That we are. And who are you?"

This had been a mistake, arriving unannounced. He turned his gaze to Beth. "I'm Anderson Warren and," he revealed the bouquet he'd been hiding, "I came to call on Beth."

The married couple exchanged a glance and a short, soft conversation. The woman who was most likely Beth's mom turned to her daughter. "Are you up for company, honey?"

Beth nodded and took a step closer. "Hi, Anderson."

"Call me Andy, please?" He now stood on the bottom step and offered the flowers. That coaxed a slight smile.

"Andy, let me introduce you to my family."

Beth swiveled and pointed to each in turn. When she was finished, the mother reached for the bouquet. "Why don't I put these in water? Anderson, would you like to join us for our evening meal? We're having a cookout."

Anderson glanced at Beth, seeking approval. She nodded slightly. "I'd like that."

Beth's dad spoke, but his expression was still stoic. "You two can sit out here if you'd like. The rest of us will be out back on the patio when you want to join us. I'll fire up the grill in a few minutes."

The teenage girl, Anderson thought her name was Missi, spoke up. "I don't mind keeping them company."

Beth's eyes went wide as she looked at her sister in horror. "I'm sure Dad will need your help."

The girl shook her head. "Nope. He can do anything and never needs me."

The mother rolled her eyes and smiled. "But I do. Missi, can you please go husk the corn? There's a dozen in the fridge."

"Mom!"

Anderson almost laughed at the expression Beth's sister gave her mother. After they all left, Beth sat on the glider. Anderson repositioned one of the porch chairs so they faced each other.

The smile had faded from Beth's lips. "I was beginning to think I wouldn't see you again."

"Why would you say that? Because I missed breakfast?"

"That was part of it. I thought maybe my comments yesterday weren't to your liking."

"Comments?"

"Come on, Andy. I shouldn't have told you how I felt. Sometimes I don't know when to keep quiet."

Despite the look of sorrow on her face, she was adorable. There was something very special about this young lady. "Well, sorry you feel that way."

"What?"

"I, for one, am glad you told me. It's refreshing to meet someone who is honest coming out of the gate."

"Gate? What are you talking about?"

He ran his hand through his hair and chuckled. "You'll have to forgive me. I live north of Cincy, which is just across the Ohio River from Louisville... Kentucky. You know, home of Churchill Downs." She seemed puzzled. "They have horse races and the whole gate thing is, well, you know..."

"I see." She rubbed her sandaled toe on the floor board. "Sorry I ruined everything."

"Beth, you didn't. You took me by surprise, that's all. I wanted to talk about it, but you know who was there. And when we got back, you were busy. I turned on a game and waited for you, but you must have gone to your room."

"I thought you were watching baseball as a way of avoiding me. And when you weren't there this morning, I knew I'd messed up."

He reached across and took her hands. "No, no you didn't. Let me explain what happened."

Anderson was surprised by the level of attention she gave him during his explanation. Usually when he talked about his work to women, he could see the boredom light come on. But not with Beth.

When he was finished, she nodded. "Thank you. Knowing you're not mad at me makes me feel much better. Again, I'm sorry about yesterday. When you said you wanted to know more about me, I should have told you about the cat I had when I was a teenager, not my philosophy on life and love."

This lady made his heart smile. He squeezed her hands before releasing them. "No. That is exactly what I wanted to know. Now it's my turn to share. What you described, that's precisely the same thing I want. You see, the relationship you illustrated between your parents sounded very familiar. That's how Gramps and Nana are. And what they have is precisely what I want." There was a growing light in her eyes. "I think there might be something special between us. Let's not rush things, but instead, how about we see where this goes naturally, I mean knowing what we *both* want out of life." He extended his hand and she quickly took it. "Deal?"

"Deal. Thanks, Andy."

"No, thank you."

It seemed as if she were about to say something else when the screen door swung open. Beth's mom stood there. Beth released him. "The burgers are almost done. Ready to join us?"

Andy stood and offered his hand to the younger girl. Beth's face was filled with a happy smile as she took it.

"We'd love to, Mrs. Espenshade." As they followed Beth's mother inside, Anderson squeezed Beth's hand. The pretty girl intertwined her fingers with his. *I see why they call this place Paradise.*

Chapter Six

After the stifling heat in the sunshine, it was only a tad bit cooler in the pavilion. At least they were in the shade. Beth rested at a bench as she waited for Anderson to return. Despite their ten-mile hike, the man with seemingly limitless energy volunteered to retrieve the picnic basket from the car. The earthy fragrance of the tall pine trees filled the air, and Beth's heart. Beth and Anderson were spending the afternoon at Caledonia State Park, north of Gettysburg.

The bounce in the man's step drew her attention as he returned with the food. Her heart whispered in her ear. *So handsome, so kind. Yep, he's the one.* But then her mind tapped her on the shoulder. *The project's over in two weeks. What will happen then?*

Anderson had a great smile. "I come bearing gifts." He quickly laid a spread on the table and dished out the food they'd prepared together earlier in the day.

"It looks scrumptious." A sudden pang of longing filled her heart. *Is it possible this will come to an end?* She extended her hand. "May I give the blessing?"

"Of course."

"God above, thank you for this meal and the wonderful man I'm sharing it with. I, no, *we* believe you brought us together... and, and..." It was becoming difficult to get the words out in a normal voice, so she stopped. Still, her voice squeaked when she finished. "Amen."

"Is everything okay? Maybe we shouldn't have pushed so hard in this heat."

"No. I'm fine. Exhausted and hot, that's all."

They ate in silence for a while. "You know, after we finish, we could soak our feet in the creek. That would cool us down. How's that sound?"

"A definite maybe."

He tilted his head slightly. "What's wrong?"

"Nothing."

"Fibber. Spill the beans."

Beth smoothed her hair. "I was just thinking... you know, about us."

"Good thoughts?"

"Mainly."

He set down his sandwich, walked around the table and sat next to her. Without a word, they leaned together and Anderson wrapped his arms around Beth. Her words were soft. "What's going to happen in two weeks?"

"I'm glad you brought it up." He released her and they were face to face. "These last six weeks have been the best of my life."

"Mine, as well."

"I don't want us to end. Do you?"

If she spoke, Beth knew her voice would quiver. She simply shook her head.

40

"Then let's devise a plan. Would you consider moving to Ohio with me?"

And leave my home? "I can't. My job's here. Besides, I love living this close to my family. This may not be where I was born or raised, but it's where I want to live my life."

"I see."

"Would you move to Lancaster?"

"It's pretty and all, but my family is waiting in Cincy. Regardless, my job takes me all over the country. Before the current assignment, I spent four months in Birmingham, Alabama. But you know, I was thinking... why don't you come along with me? I'd work during the days, but at night, we could explore whatever area we were in... together."

A cold chill ascended her spine. *Like living together?* "And what would I do while you're at work?"

He looked down and away. "Guess I hadn't thought it through."

"That doesn't sound like a fun way to live. Suppose someday we'd get married and have children? Would you drag them along, too?"

"Of course not. By then, I'm hoping to move up in the company. They have regional offices across the country. We might have our pick of where to live."

It was all too apparent. *He doesn't feel the same as I do.* "Your job's really important to you, isn't it? Cleaning up old factories."

"I see it as saving the environment... for the next generation."

The fairy tale was ending. "Maybe this isn't going to work out like I hoped."

Anderson changed position so he could study her. "What do you mean?"

"I was hoping things would kind of like continue the way they've been going. But if you leave..." *This is fruitless.* She looked away.

Anderson gently grasped her chin and turned her head so she faced him. "Please don't stop talking. I want you to be honest with me."

"I've never been anything but truthful with you."

The man fidgeted as he sat next to her. "Beth, I've been with this company since I graduated from college and worked hard to earn my position as a Project Manager. Hopefully, the next rung will land me someplace where I'm not on the road all the time. It's so close I can almost touch it."

Despite the ambient temperature of the air, a chill swept over her. "I understand how significant your job is to you." *Much more important than I'll ever be.* Beth stood and walked to a corner of the pavilion. *God, this hurts.* She was trying to hold it in, but the proof was on her cheeks.

Anderson appeared in front of her, trying to wipe away her tears. "Beth..."

"Don't worry. I won't stand in your way."

He released a heavy sigh. "I'm not sure this is going to be worth it."

A knife in the back wouldn't have hurt as badly. "I understand. You're on the way up the ladder, and making your dreams come true. And me? I'm just an obstacle to your career path."

Anderson gently touched her face. His eyes were watery as well. "Stop. I won't allow anything to come between us."

She had to sniff before she spoke. "It already has. In two weeks, you'll wave goodbye and—"

"No!" He grasped her hands, tightly. "This is stupid. You're the best thing to ever happen to me. I'll quit if I have to."

"This is your career. You love what you do."

"I love you more."

What? "You... did you just say you love me?"

He stood a little taller now. "Yes, I do. I love you, Beth. You stole my heart that day on your parents' porch. That's when I first realized I'd fallen for you. Please tell me you feel the same."

Feelings she'd never known before made her chest feel light. "Yes. I love you, too. That first day when you walked into the inn, I knew you were my destiny."

Anderson leaned in, tilting his head. Beth's lips met him halfway for their first kiss. Closing her eyes, images of waves caressing the shore filled her mind. The warm water wrapped around Beth and Anderson as they held each other.

They were both breathing heavily. Anderson spoke first. "Because of my past, I fought the emotion. But I can't help myself. I'm totally in love with you. I don't want to hide it anymore."

The warmth in her chest was increasing, but the situation wasn't yet resolved. "So, there we have it. But what do we do?"

His steel blue eyes now blazed as his smile grew. "It's time to express my love for you, in actions, not just words."

***

The magical touch of her hand in his made it hard to concentrate enough to drive. *I can't believe this happened to me.* This afternoon, he and Beth had talked heart to heart, expressing their hopes and dreams and most importantly, their desire for a future. Together, as in forever. As if they were one, they'd come up with a plan.

"We should probably think about supper."

He chanced a glance at his companion. Those lips displayed a smile, but her eyes revealed more. *This is what forever looks like.* "Where do you want to go?"

"Maybe we can get takeout. I'm planning on making cinnamon rolls for breakfast."

"Ooh, can you put some slivered almonds in them?"

"I try not to put nuts in the food I prepare because so many people have allergies these days, but... I could make you a private batch. Would you like that... darling?"

If he smiled any wider, his teeth would fall out. "Only if you'll share them with me, honey."

The shadows were getting long as they crossed the bridge over the Susquehanna River. Beth squeezed his hand. "See that old bridge over there?"

"Um-hmm."

"I remember the first time I saw it. That was in the old days, when Mom and I didn't see eye to eye.

Actually, we fought like cats and dogs. I was mad because she moved us from Oklahoma and relocated Missi and me more times than I could count. I made some rude comment about how I hated this area."

"Wait. I thought you loved it here."

"I do, now. Back then, I hated most everything. But Mom simply reached across the seat and squeezed my hand. 'Everything will be fine. I bet you might even find peace and happiness right here in this place they call Paradise'. I rejected her words then, but looking back, she was right." Beth raised his hand to her lips. "I found you."

Anderson couldn't contain his laughter. "She is pretty smart. In fact, I've never known your mom to be wrong."

"I'm glad it's you."

The big SUV swerved as he reached across the console for a kiss.

"What are you hungry for tonight?"

"I'm in the mood for shrimp fried rice, if it's okay with you."

I would eat mud pies just to be with you. "Sounds perfect. Want to call our order in and we can pick it up on the way?"

"I have a counter-proposal. Why don't you drop me off at the inn before you pick it up? That way, I'll be finished by the time you get back." Beth had reached across and took his hand. "I have a bottle of white wine in my cooler upstairs. Perhaps we could have a picnic under the stars?"

"That sounds great, except for one thing."

Her giggle was silly and sweet. "And that is?"

"I want to be by your side, every second."

She didn't answer, so he took a split second to glance her way. Beth was glowing. "That's what forever is for."

Chapter Seven

The morning breeze carried the scent of happiness... well, actually it was bacon and cinnamon rolls if specificity was required. The woman he loved looked so pretty this morning, in her denim capris and white, Egyptian cotton tunic. But the thing of beauty was her smile, evidenced both on those sweet lips and in her expressive eyes.

Beth finally made her way to his table and sat next to him. "Good morning, Mr. Warren. Would you care for some coffee to go along with cinnamon buns and bacon this morning?"

It was just the two of them, but he still kept his voice low. "Will you sweeten my coffee with your kisses?"

"Not in front of the customers, but I'm sure we can work something out when you come home tonight."

Anderson offered his hand, which Beth quickly took. He still maintained a low volume on his voice. "Father, we thank you for this food and the hands that prepared it. And I want to send a special prayer of thanksgiving for bringing us together, and helping us find our way yesterday. In the gospel of Mark, You promised that what You brought together, no man could put asunder. We thank You for helping us find each other."

Beth squeezed his hand tightly. "Amen."

The pastry seemed to melt in his mouth. "Good Lord, this is scrumptious. Where'd you learn to bake like this?"

"My mom. I inherited a lot from her."

"Obviously more than just her good looks."

Beth feigned surprise, but he saw right through it. "You were checking out my mom?"

"They say you should take a good look at the mother, because that's who the girl will resemble someday."

"Anderson Warren!"

She was so wonderful. "All kidding aside, no lady could ever move me like you do. You're the most beautiful woman God ever created."

She nodded as she took a bite of her roll. "Nice recovery."

Anderson was reaching for another roll when he saw Beth set her pastry down and then wipe her face with a napkin. "Good morning. May I help you?"

"Nah, I think I found what I'm looking for."

The coffee in his mouth turned to bile. *I recognize that voice.* Standing as he whipped around, Anderson found himself face-to-face with the girl who burned him—Michaela.

***

Beth noticed the woman as she traipsed up the steps. She wore knee-high boots with stiletto heels, a *very* short skirt and a near see-through, tight white shirt. Right away, Beth knew the woman was in the wrong place.

"Good morning. May I help you?"

The denigrating response irritated Beth, but that wasn't what bothered her. Instead, it was the bright red of Anderson's face. He immediately faced the girl.

"What are you doing here?"

"Isn't that a fine way to greet your fiancée?"

Did she say fiancée? Beth became conscious that all the other guests had turned to take in the spectacle.

"Ex, Michaela, ex-fiancée."

The woman noticed Beth watching intently. Michaela shot her a wink. "Andy loves to role play. He pretends we're not together, so when we make up, we have great—"

"Shut up and get out of here." Andy's voice was high and if his face turned any darker, Beth was afraid he might pass out.

Anderson's angry reaction to the woman concerned Beth. This was a side of him she hadn't known existed.

"Oh, Andy. I missed you. It was hard to find you this time."

"That's because I didn't want *you* to ever find me."

The woman placed her hands on her hips and shook her head. "Whoa! Where'd that come from? Maybe you should talk to a doctor about your episodes of anger. They seem to appear from nowhere. I don't know why you got so upset."

"Walking in on my you and catching you... doing, you know what. Isn't that reason enough?" he asked.

"Don't act so high and mighty. As if you never played around. Now, you're pretending to be a choir boy in front of everyone, aren't you?"

Beth felt physically ill, but the worst pain was in her chest. She knew her heart was splitting right in two. She needed to do something, but didn't immediately know how to handle this incident. That's when her training on dealing with difficult people and situations kicked in.

Anderson's voice was increasing in volume. "Why can't you leave me alone? We're over, do you get that? Over, over, over!"

Beth moved until she stood between them. "I need to ask both of you to move this off the porch and into the drive. You're causing a commotion and interrupting my customers' breakfast. Please stop this before I'm forced to take drastic actions."

The woman shoved Beth back into her chair. "Butt out, this is a private discussion."

Anderson grabbed the woman's arm, pulled her away from Beth and screamed, "Leave me alone!"

Snatching the pot of coffee from the table, Michaela threw it at Anderson. He ducked and the hot liquid hit Beth in the face.

Two of the male guests responded and separated Anderson and the girl who claimed to be his fiancée. The screaming match continued. Beth had no choice. She yanked her cell from her pocket and punched in Henry Campbell's number. The husband of the Bed & Breakfast's owner, Henry was a former Royal Marine.

Beth glanced at the ongoing altercation. Henry would know what do. Lord knows Beth didn't have a clue.

***

Anderson sat behind the wheel of his SUV in the B&B lot, trying to determine his next action. Michaela's insanity escalated to the point that even Henry Campbell couldn't control her. He had to call the police. The officers eventually drove away with his ex in the back of the police car, after she admitted to them—in front of Mr. Campbell—that this was premediated on her part to shame Anderson. And she had.

The knock on his window startled him. Mr. Campbell was standing outside. "Yes, sir?"

Henry motioned with his head in the direction of the road. "It's time to leave, Mr. Warren."

"This wasn't my fault. Michaela even admitted that."

"She did, but you disrupted the solitude for my other guests as well as my manager. I won't put up with that, and I don't want Beth to feel uncomfortable, so hit the road. As in now."

"You don't understand. I need to talk to Beth. I love her, Mr. Campbell."

Anderson noted the red color spreading across Mr. Campbell's face. The man's words were measured and menacing. "Let me make this perfectly obvious to you. You will not return here or bother Beth Rutledge again. If you do, you will answer to me. Is that clear?"

"Yes, sir." With his tail between his legs, Anderson left the Campbell property. But before he exited, he'd searched the lot for Beth's Explorer. It was gone. Anderson knew she would head for her mother's house. He slowed to allow a work buggy to turn into a farm lane. *I can't let it end like this.* He should be at the project, but what was more important... a career or Beth?

There really was no decision to be made. His hands were shaking as the Espenshade home came into view. Yep, there it was. Her red Explorer was parked out front. *I've got to make this right.* He couldn't just walk away, not from Beth.

Jumping out of the cab, he raced for the front porch. Anderson stopped dead in his tracks when he saw who was sitting on the top step. Her dad, Sam, had a glass of tea in one hand and held his cane in the other. The expression on the man's face wasn't pleasant.

"Is Beth here?"

"Good morning to you too, Mr. Warren."

"Where are my manners? Good morning, Mr. Espenshade. May I see Beth?"

"She's busy."

"Please sir, it's important."

"The answer is... no."

I'll go crazy if it ends like this. Maybe if he called out to her, she'd come out of the house. "Beth? Beth, are you in there? I need to speak with you." Anderson stepped to the side, planning on sneaking past Mr. Espenshade.

Beth's step-father struggled to his feet and extended his cane until it touched Anderson's chest. "I'm beginning to think you don't understand English. Let me make this easy for you. I want you to leave, *now*."

"I just want to have a few words with Beth. You don't understand."

The other man grasped his cane with both hands, holding it like a baseball bat. "I understand that you hurt my daughter. Beth doesn't want to talk to you. Leave now, or perhaps you need an incentive." Mr. Espenshade curled the cane over his shoulder and seemed prepared to use it to strike Anderson.

Holding his hands in front of him, Anderson stepped back to the ground. "I'm sorry. I wasn't trying to be difficult. I just need to speak to Beth. If I don't, I'll go insane."

Her step-dad dropped down to the next lower stair, maintaining his place between Anderson and the porch. "That ship has sailed, son."

Son? I'm older than you. It was an effort not to lose his temper like he'd done with the crazy woman earlier. "Okay. I understand. Maybe if she wouldn't mind, I'll come back and stop by to chat with her tomorrow."

Espenshade had reached the ground and continued walking toward Anderson. "Not a good idea. And just so you don't get any wild thoughts, I'm taking some time off to spend with my daughter. You know, in case she needs me."

Anderson's back was now against the grill of his ride. He was out of options and in no way did he wish to start a fight with her step-father. He'd lost. This was the worst day of his life.

"I'm sorry to have bothered you, Mr. Espenshade. I'm really not a jerk or a stalker. I'll leave now and I promise you I won't be a bother to Beth. But before I go, could you do me a favor?"

The younger man lowered the cane, but it was still at the ready. "What's that?"

"Please let Beth know that I love her. If she ever wants to talk about this morning or our future, all she needs to do is call. I mean, any time of the day or night." He stopped, assessing the other man. But Sam Espenshade's expression hadn't changed.

Beth's dad motioned to the vehicle. "I'll pass your message on to her. Perhaps it's best if you leave now."

Any hope he'd had was fading. "The ball's in her court, but I hope she reaches out to me. You see, I screwed up, Mr. Espenshade. I love your daughter with all my soul. I hope she has it in her heart to forgive me for something that wasn't even my fault." There were more words in his heart he wanted to say, but he might as well have been talking to a brick wall.

"Goodbye, Anderson."

"And to you as well, sir." Anderson took one last glance at the house. Maybe it was his imagination, but he could have sworn he caught a glimpse of Beth watching from the front door just before the curtain closed.

***

Her step-dad walked in the door, hung his cane on the back of the kitchen chair and reached for her. Beth allowed Sam to hold her tight. Other warm arms, those belonging to her mom, encompassed her. Everything grew blurry.

"Did he leave?"

She felt Sam nod. "I did like you asked me to. I made him go."

Beth rubbed her nose with the back of her hand. "It was for the best, wasn't it?"

With a deep sigh, Sam replied, "I'm not so sure. I truly believe he loves you, and can tell you love him. Mom and I have known that for a while."

Her mom kissed the side of her head before releasing Beth. "Sam, do you mind giving Beth and me a few minutes?"

"Oh, okay. I'll be on the porch if you need me."

Beth nodded. "Thanks, Dad."

Hannah brewed two cups of tea in the Keurig and placed them on the table. Beth sniffed and looked her mom in the eyes. "Did I make a mistake?"

The older woman shrugged her shoulders. "Only you can answer that."

"Anderson never mentioned he'd been engaged."

"I see."

"And then the way he acted with her. His anger shocked me. Suppose that was me on the receiving end? That's not the kind of life I want."

Hannah touched her shoulder. "I understand."

"He was the one I wanted for life. I dreamed about us getting married, having kids, spending forever together."

"I know you did."

"Is it asking too much to expect a happy, peaceful existence with a family, and a lifetime romance?"

"Honey, you're young. Sometimes we have to wait a long time for dreams to come true."

"But you didn't have to wait. You got married at seventeen."

Looking away, Hannah replied, "My marriage to your father wasn't a fairy tale."

That's strange. "Wait, you and Dad, I mean my real father, were happy, weren't you?"

"Yes, in certain ways, however, you didn't see the full picture."

"Do you regret marrying him?"

"No, but that relationship wasn't anything like what Sam and I have."

"Okay, but when you and Sam met, it seemed like everything just fell in place, right?"

Hannah's eyes were filled with compassion and understanding. "No. One thing after another got in our way and threatened to drive us apart. Sam's temper and immaturity were a big problem. Things got so bad, I had to let Sam go. I'm sure you remember. But we eventually got back together."

"But if Sam's actions were enough to make you split, why did you take him back?"

"I believe God destined us to be together. But it was in His time, not ours. There were parts of His master plan that weren't yet in place."

Beth understood what her mom was telling her, but that didn't make the pain any less. "Will there ever be a time for Andy and me?"

Hannah shrugged. "I don't know. Only time will tell."

Chapter Eight

Beth sat in the swing in the side yard. The late autumn sky seemed ready to spit drizzle on the withered flower beds. Little boy voices carried over the wind from the neighboring house. The sons of Sophie Miller were playing a game of tag in the back yard. *What would it be like to have a family?*

A man's face appeared before her. It belonged to the man she had wanted to share her dreams. *Where are you tonight, Andy?* He'd sent her a long letter, explaining and confessing about Michaela and everything else that he'd ever done. He'd told her the next move was up to her. But Beth waited for a sign, one that hadn't come.

The slamming of the screen door broke her concentration. Little sister Missi stepped from the porch carrying two cups and a plastic bag. Beth could see wisps of vapor roll from the top of the mugs. One thing about it, Missi and Beth had drawn even closer since Andy's departure. Missi occasionally stayed with Beth during the week and kept her company every lonely weekend.

"Brought you some hot chocolate." She handed Beth the cup and offered the plastic bag. "Mom sent along some oatmeal cookies."

"Thanks." They ate their snacks in silence. *These were Andy's favorite.* Try as she might, Beth had never been able to get him out of her mind. So much so that she was sure she was hallucinating. Beth had even thought she'd seen him in the area lately. *Right. He moved on and is probably off on some other assignment.*

"Are we going home for dinner tonight?"

Beth shook her head to disperse the thoughts. "Of course. I have a couple arriving today. They're late but should be here soon, I hope. After I get them checked in, we can head home. Mom texted me that she made ham and bean soup for dinner."

"That's not my favorite meal. Good thing we've got cookies." Missi again reached into the bag and extracted two whoopie pies with light brown cakes. "See what I've got? I took them when Mom wasn't looking. They're pumpkin flavored."

Beth shook her head and then laughed. "You are aware Mom knows when you take these, aren't you?"

Missi winked. "Maybe."

The roar of a loud motor was carried by the wind. Beth gazed at the road and watched as an old lime green car slowed down and then turned into the parking lot. Beth handed the remainder of her snack to Missi. "Maybe these are our guests. Here, finish mine and as soon as I get them checked in, we'll hit the road."

Beth covered the short distance to the porch. A thin man sporting a halo of grey hair helped a pretty older woman from the car. Beth couldn't miss how they held hands as they mounted the stairs. *You can see they're in love.* Beth forced a smile. "Are you the Franklins?"

The woman giggled. "For the last fifty-four years. And you are?"

Extending her hand, she answered, "I'm the manager, Beth Rutledge."

The pair exchanged a quick smile before the man said, "I'm Paul and I'd like to apologize for our tardiness. Old Bessy," he motioned over his shoulder at the green car, "developed a miss. We had a hard time finding someone who could work on a six-pack."

"Six-pack? Are you talking about beer? I'm not sure I understand."

The lady laughed. "He's talking about the car. It's over fifty years old."

He released the woman's hand and placed his on his hips. Despite that, Beth could tell he was filled with mirth. "We bought that car together." He turned to Beth. "That 'car' as Belinda calls it, is a 1970 Dodge Challenger Trans Am or T/A for short. She has the original 340-cubic-inch engine with three two-barrel carburetors, also known as a six-pack. Nineteen-seventy was the only year Chrysler made them. Fastest car on the road."

Belinda nodded. "That's right. She'll pass anything... but a gas station."

Beth stifled a laugh. The old couple was adorable. "I see. Come in and I'll get your room key. Are you going to do anything special or are you just here to do sight-seeing?"

Paul answered for them. "We came to town for a specific event."

"Really? What event?"

Her back was turned, but Beth could have sworn she heard a smacking sound. When she turned around, Paul was rubbing his arm. The woman smiled. "It's a private, family thing. However, we also want to do some sight-seeing. Beth, would you mind being our tour guide tomorrow afternoon?"

Beth shrugged. "Sure, why not. Anything in particular you want to see?"

Again, the pair shared a knowing smile. Paul seemed about ready to break out in a laugh. "The Strasburg Railroad."

***

Despite the half-century of age, the interior of the Challenger looked and smelled as if it had just rolled out of the showroom. Beth was enjoying her day with the Franklins. Leaving just after Beth cleaned up from breakfast, she had directed the couple through rural Lancaster County on a quest to see covered bridges. The sole detraction of the ride had been the loudness of the exhaust system.

The pair's kindness reminded her of her step-father Sam's parents. Gentle, funny and obviously in love, they had treated her more like a granddaughter than as the stranger she was. *A love just like theirs is what I want when I'm as old as the Franklins.*

"Look, there's a sign for Strasburg." Belinda turned in the seat, raising her voice to be heard over the mufflers. "Is the railroad down here?"

Beth spoke loudly. "When we get to the square, we'll turn left."

Paul checked his watch. "Isn't there a big train layout close by?"

"The Choo-Choo Barn is right next to the actual Strasburg Railroad."

Belinda nodded quickly. "Yeah, let's go there."

Paul parked the old Dodge well away from other vehicles, as he'd done everywhere they went. After the old man helped his wife from the front seat, he offered a hand to Beth so she could exit. "Since we invited you, it's our treat."

Beth protested. "I couldn't, really. I'll purchase my own admission."

Belinda held up some papers. "Oh look, I already have three tickets."

What? "When did you get those?"

Paul nudged his elbow gently into her ribs. "We saw them online and bought them a while ago. They're cheaper when you buy ahead."

"But why did you get three tickets?"

The woman's face turned pink. "I'm forgetful sometimes. Guess I miscounted."

"Oh, okay." That didn't seem right, but Beth went in with them.

The couple appeared to be quite intrigued with the setup, but Beth noted they paid close attention to their wrist watches. About halfway around the platform, they turned to her.

Paul spoke, "What say we head over to the Strasburg Railroad? I heard it's called the 'Road to Paradise'."

"That's correct, but the train only runs on weekends this time of year. Today's Thursday."

Belinda put her hand to her cheek. "Is that a fact?"

Beth couldn't help but laugh at the woman's expression. "It is."

Paul shot her a weird look. "We must have our wires crossed because we also purchased tickets for the train. For today and look," he displayed a boarding pass, "it says the train leaves in fifteen minutes. And I can't believe it. We have an extra ticket. You can have it."

Beth examined the paper. It appeared Paul was correct. The pass did indicate a departure in just a few minutes... this very day. "That's peculiar."

"Come on, ladies. We better hurry."

They got in the car and Paul fired up the old hot rod. But when he got to the railroad's parking lot, Paul parked next to a much newer version of the Franklins' car. The newer vehicle was the exact color of the older couple's auto. Every other place, he'd avoided parking around other vehicles, Beth was curious. "Is that car also a Challenger?"

Paul nodded. "Yep. It's just newer, that's all. Not as fast or as cool as ours."

As Beth walked away, she noticed both Dodges had Ohio license plates. *What a coincidence.* There were only a handful of vehicles in the lot. When her eyes fell on the van, she stopped.

Belinda and Paul turned to her. "Is something the matter?"

"T-th-that's my mom's car. See that Disney World bumper sticker? I put it on there. And there's my Uncle Mickey's Jeep. And Sam's parents' car and I recognize all the other vehicles as well."

"Huh. Why would they all be here?"

"I don't have a clue. Wait. You two... you are involved in this. What's happening?"

Belinda walked over and took Beth's hand. The lady was all smiles. "Come along, dearie. We'll find out together."

I don't understand this, at all. The conductor stood on the ground at the stairs to the dining car. He also sported a large smile. "All aboard!"

Paul helped his wife onto the stairs before offering his hand to Beth. "After you, princess."

Princess? What's going on? Is this a party? Beth's birthday had passed two months ago with little fanfare. Another conductor stood at the door to the dining car. The man grinned and held the door open.

Beth swallowed hard before entering. The rolling stock was full, but everybody was facing away from her. Then when she'd only taken two steps, Mr. Franklin called out. Almost as one, all the passengers pivoted and faced her. The noise reverberated when they yelled, "Surprise!"

In shock, Beth looked at the people who were there. Her mom, Sam, Missi, Sam's parents, Aunt Riley, Uncle Mickey, Eileen and Josh Miller, Terry Faughtinger, Henry and Ellie Campbell, Luke and Didi Zinn, Anderson... *Anderson?* Her mouth fell open.

"Andy?" Beth pinched her leg to make sure she wasn't dreaming.

He walked up and held out his hands. Beth grasped them, tightly. "It's really you. What are you doing here?"

He'd never looked as happy. "Beth, I can't live without you. I moved to Lancaster months ago to be close to you."

"But you never called. What's happening?"

"Your mom said you were waiting for a sign." He paused for a second or two. "This is it."

"Wait, you talked to my mom?"

"I've been in contact with your parents since the day I left. They helped me understand what I did wrong and suggested how to correct it. You're lucky to have such loving parents who only want what's best for you."

Beth's head was spinning. "I don't know what to say."

He winked at her. "I see you met Gramps and Nana... Franklin?"

"That's who they are?"

"Yep. And if you're wondering how your parents, family and friends got here... well, I invited them. After getting permission from your parents, I sprung this idea on them. Your mom even helped me plan today."

"Permission for what?"

"This." Anderson dropped to his knee and pulled a box from his pocket. Anderson cleared his throat. "Bethany Rutledge. You and I were meant to be. You know we both want the same thing—a love like your mom and Sam have... A love like my Gramps and Nana. Beth, I want to spend my life with you. The bad and the good. Sad times and happy. Together, let's make our own fairy tale. Will you share your life with me, as my wife?"

She could barely nod. "You know that's what I want."

The deep voice of the conductor split the air. "All aboard! Welcome to the Strasburg Railroad, heading to Paradise and all points beyond."

Anderson's lips met hers. After he drew away, Beth laughed.

"What's so funny?"

"Did you hear what he said?"

"No, what?"

"Heading to Paradise. If that's where we're going, they can stop now, because I'm already there." Their lips met again and everything faded away. This truly was paradise.

The End

Enjoyed this book?

Please consider placing a review on Amazon!
This will help other readers find great books.

*Get exclusive
never-before-published content!*

A Paradise Short Story

Download your free copy of
Skating in Paradise today!

Other Books by this Author

Seeking Forever (Book 1)

Kaitlin Jenkins long ago gave up the notion of ever finding true love, let alone a soulmate. Jeremy is trying to get his life back on track after a bitter divorce and an earlier than planned departure from the military. They have nothing in common, except their distrust of the opposite sex.

Seeking Happiness (Book 2)

Kelly was floored when her husband of ten years announced he was leaving her for another woman. But she isn't ready to be an old maid. And she soon discovers there's no shortage of men waiting in line.

Seeking Eternity (Book 3)

At eighteen, Nora Thomas fell in love with her soulmate and best friend, Stan Jenkins. But Nora was already engaged to a wonderful man, so reluctantly, Nora told Stan they could only be friends. Stan completely disappeared (well, almost), from her world, from her life, from everywhere but Nora's broken heart.

Seeking the Pearl (Book 4)

Eleanor Lucia has lived a sad and somber life, until she travels to London to open a hotel for her Aunt Kaitlin. For that's where Ellie meets Scotsman Henry Campbell and finally discovers true happiness. All that changes when Ellie disappears without a trace and everyone believes she is dead. Well, almost everyone.

Whispers in Paradise (Book 1)

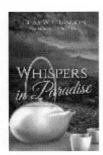

Ashley never expected to find love, not after what cancer had done to her body. Until Harry Campbell courts her in a fairy tale romance that exceeds even her wildest dreams. But all that changes in an instant when Harry's youngest brother steals a kiss, and Harry walks in on it.

Echoes in Paradise (Book 2)

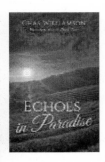

Hannah Rutledge rips her daughters from their Oklahoma home in the middle of the night to escape a predator from her youth. After months of secrecy and frequent moves to hide her trail, she settles in Paradise and ends up working with Sam Espenshade, twelve years her junior. Sam wins her daughters' hearts, and earns her friendship, but because of her past, can she ever totally trust anyone again?

Courage in Paradise (Book 3)

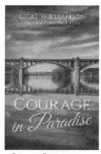

Sportscaster Riley Espenshade returns to southcentral Pennsylvania so she can be close to her family while growing her career. One thing Riley didn't anticipate was falling for hockey's greatest superstar, Mickey Campeau, a rough and tall Canadian who always gets what he wants... and that happens to be Riley. Total bliss seems to be at her fingertips, until she discovers Mickey also loves another girl.

Stranded in Paradise (Book 4)

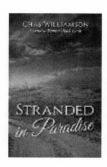

When Aubrey Stettinger is attacked on a train, a tall, handsome stranger comes to her assistance, but disappears just as quickly. Four months later, Aubrey finds herself recuperating in Paradise at the home of a friend of a friend.

When she realizes the host's brother is the hero from the train, she suspects their reunion is more than a coincidence. Slowly, and for the first time in her life, Aubrey begins to trust—in family, in God and in a man. But just when she's ready to let her guard down, life once again reminds her she can't trust anyone. Caught between two worlds, Aubrey must choose between chasing her fleeting dreams and carving out a new life in this strange place.

Christmas in Paradise (Book 5)

True love never dies, except when it abandons you at the altar. Rachel Domitar has found the man of her dreams. The church is filled with friends and family, her hair and dress are perfect, and the honeymoon beckons, but one knock at the door is about to change everything.

Homecoming in Paradise (Book 6)

Dreams do come true, but is fame worth the steep price of success? For six years, Margaret Campbell has toiled to make the Scottish Lass Winery of Paradise a reality. And finally, her dream is within reach. But while she's been away, everything has changed. The close-knit family of her memory might as well be a bunch of strangers. And when she discovers the neighbor's children look exactly like her brother Henry, she suspects her family's values have been breached.

Treasure in Paradise (Book 7)

After an unexpected admonishment from her editor, Jasmine Blue travels to Lancaster County, Pennsylvania, to research her new book. Taking the name Eileen Nussbaum to hide her true identity, she discovers a wealth of rich and quirky characters, good fodder for the next novel. But one man, Josh Miller, has her intrigued. Though obviously talented, he seems to ignore his gifts. Then when Jasmine uncovers Josh's real secret, she's drawn to him in a way she's never felt before.

Hayride in Paradise (Novella)

They live in two separate worlds. Rebecca is Amish and Abraham is English, but the attraction between them is undeniable. Can they overcome their differences to find true love?

About the Author

Chas Williamson's lifelong dream was to write. He started writing his first book at age eight, but quit after two paragraphs. Yet some dreams never fade...

It's said one should write what one knows best. That left two choices—the world of environmental health and safety... or romance. Chas and his bride have built a fairytale life of love. At her encouragement, he began writing romance. The characters you'll meet in his books are very real to him, and he hopes they'll become just as real to you.

True Love Lasts Forever!

Follow Chas on
www.bookbub.com/authors/chas-williamson